MIGHTY READER

AND THE BIG FREEZE

Will Hillenbrand

HOLIDAY HOUSE · NEW YORK

To Therese, a Mighty Teacher

Copyright © 2019 by Will Hillenbrand

All Rights Reserved

HOLIDAY HOUSE is registered in the U.S. Patent and Trademark Office.

Printed and bound in November 2018 at Tien Wah Press, Johor Bahru, Johor, Malaysia.

The artwork was created with pixel media.

www.holidayhouse.com

First Edition

1 3 5 7 9 10 8 6 4 2

Library of Congress CIP is available.

ISBN: 978-0-8234-3992-8 (hardcover)

The bus driver closed the door.

SLAM!

Hugo looked for an empty seat.

Ms. Wulff introduced Hugo to the class by reading a book called *Friends*.

Hugo read a book to the class that he had made at home.

Barkley asked if he could be Hugo's lunch buddy.

Hugo saw that Barkley was in big trouble.

But he knew just what to do.

DRESS-UP CENTER

Meanwhile, a reading emergency erupted.

Oh, no! Lockjaw!

Zephyr covered her eyes.

Comet chased his tail.

Bronte almost got sick.

Inky howled.

Mighty Reader scanned the cubbies with his X-ray vision. He found Barkley's favorite book.

Faster than the eye could see, he was back in the group.

Mighty Reader held the book in front of Barkley to remind him that he was a reader.

He hoped that it would give Barkley's sagging confidence a boost.

But was it too late? His friend was freezing up.

He kept right on reading by acting out the pictures.

"SNORE!" replied Bear.

Faster than the eye could see,
and without anyone noticing,
Mighty Reader was gone.

Hugo was back in the group.

DRESS-UP
CENTER

No one spotted that the author had arrived.

Barkley had a question.

Oh, I hit bumps along the way; that's normal. Mistakes often help me see how to make my work better.

Mole took a deep breath and wiped his eyes.

Ready, OFF WE GO!

Wobble,
Wobble,
Wobble . . .

There are many ways to make a story, but for me the pictures always come first.

Then he read.

Back on the bus, Barkley was holding the glossy new book.